A TALL, TALL GIANT

Printed in the U.S.A. P.O. Box 193 Provo, Utah 84603

ISBN 0-89868-431-5–Library Bound
ISBN 0-89868-432-3–Soft Bound
ISBN 0-89868-433-1-Trade

A PREDICTABLE WORD BOOK

A TALL, TALL GIANT

Story by Janie Spaht Gill, Ph.D.
Illustrations by Elisabeth Lambson

 ARO PUBLISHING

A Tall, tall giant,

went through a tall,
tall gate,

across a tall, tall porch,

through a tall, tall door,

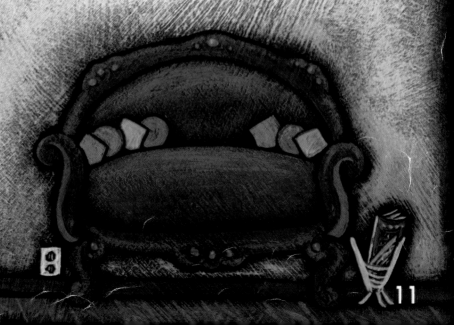

11

into a tall, tall house,

down a tall, tall hall,

15

up some tall, tall steps,

into a tall, tall attic,

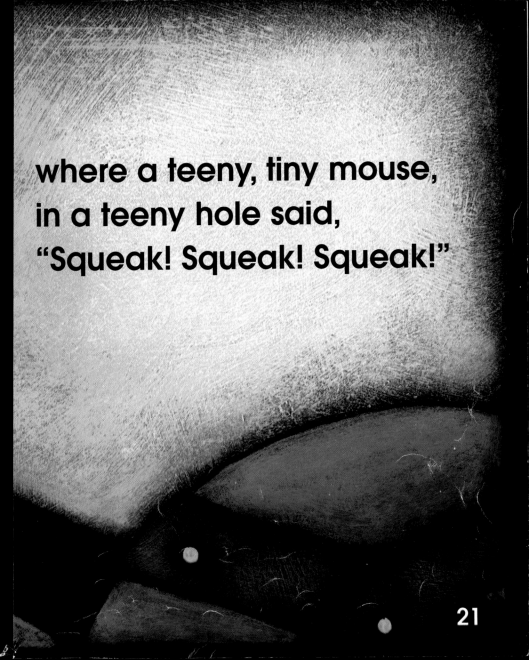

where a teeny, tiny mouse,
in a teeny hole said,
"Squeak! Squeak! Squeak!"

"E-e-k!" said the tall, tall man, as he ran, tripping over his feet.